STERLING CHILDREN'S BOOKS
New York

An Imprint of Sterling Publishing Co., Inc.
1166 Avenue of the Americas
New York, NY 10036

© 2017 by Kristyna Litten

Published by arrangement with
Simon & Schuster UK Ltd.

ISBN 978-1-4549-2499-9

Distributed in Canada by Sterling Publishing Co., Inc.
c/o Canadian Manda Group, 664 Annette Street
Toronto, Ontario, Canada M6S 2C8

For information about custom editions, special sales, and premium
and corporate purchases, please contact Sterling Special Sales
at 800-805-5489 or specialsales@sterlingpublishing.com.

Manufactured in China
Lot #:
2 4 6 8 10 9 7 5 3 1
12/16

www.sterlingpublishing.com

TO DĚDA AND GRANDAD
—K. L.

NORTON AND Alpha

by Kristyna Litten

STERLING CHILDREN'S BOOKS
New York

Norton was a collector.
Battered wheels, rusty cogs, broken springs—
they all found their way into Norton's collection.

But best of all were the things Norton *didn't* have a name for.

Norton found interesting things almost everywhere he looked.

They were rarely beautiful, but they were usually useful.

And from what he found,
big or small,
Norton made the most
amazing inventions.

One day, Norton found something interesting he couldn't name.

He attached it to his latest project . . .

and then stood back.

It was PERFECT!

Norton decided to call the project ALPHA.

WOOF!

Now Norton had a companion to help with his collecting.

Alpha would follow his little robot nose down unknown paths.

He dug holes, scurried into small, unreachable places,
delved into unexplored spaces . . .

. . . and found all sorts of wonderful things.

One Tuesday morning,
Alpha's nose felt slightly odd.
It tickled and tingled and led him
to something **very** unusual.

Norton was baffled.
It was unlike anything
they had ever seen before.

What was it?

WOOF!

Norton and Alpha were determined to find out.

So, with a bit of effort, they plucked it from the ground . . .

. . . and set off on their way home.

Norton held onto his new treasure tightly.

He didn't
take his eyes
off it
for a moment,
except
to climb
the ladder
up to
his house.

Norton went straight to his workshop.

STUDYING THE UNKNOWN

He did all his usual experiments.
He oiled it.

He tried plugging it in.

He even X-rayed it.

But the results just confused Norton even more.

His new discovery
didn't seem useful
at all.

It also didn't look nearly as interesting

as it had when they first
found it.

So Norton
threw it
out the
window.

For the rest of the day, Norton and Alpha
cleaned up the mess left over from
their experiments.

They found a
little round something
their mysterious discovery
had left behind.

Norton decided to keep it.
Maybe one day he would find
a use for it.

On Wednesday,
the weather was much too wet
to go out collecting.

But Alpha still needed his exercise!

On Thursday,
it was extremely hot.
Norton and Alpha spent
most of the day trying
to keep cool.

But Friday was a perfect day for treasure hunting.
The weather was glorious. So Norton made sure they had a hearty breakfast.

They ran to the doors
and flung them open.

Then he oiled their joints
and got everything ready for
a long day's collecting.

Norton and Alpha bounced and jumped in the colorful field.

They collected lots of the blue, pink, and orange things and carried them home.

Beautiful!

And what they saw was . . .

Norton stopped trying to figure out what they were for.
All that really mattered . . .

. . . is that they made him smile!